When a DRAGON moves in AGAIN

Written by Jodi Moore   Illustrated by Howard McWilliam

Flash
Light PRESS

Library of Congress Control Number:
2014944953

Hardcover ISBN: 978-1-936261-35-2
ePDF ISBN: 9781936261536
EPUB ISBN: 9781936261543
Mobipocket ISBN: 9781936261550

Editor: Shari Dash Greenspan
Graphic Design: The Virtual Paintbrush

This book was typeset in Aunt Mildred.
The illustrations were drawn with pencil
on paper, and painted digitally.

Distributed by IPG.

Flashlight Press
527 Empire Blvd. • Brooklyn, NY 11225
www.FlashlightPress.com

For Larry,
Alex & Steve,
with love
always
–JM

For little
Rufus and his
littler brother
Miles –HM

Only tinier,

and droolier,

and stinkier.

And he'll cry. A *lot*.

Luckily, you and your dragon can entertain him.

First, you'll show off your bowling skills.

If you help your dad build a castle,
a dragon will move in.

He'll settle in all cozy and
peep at you from inside...

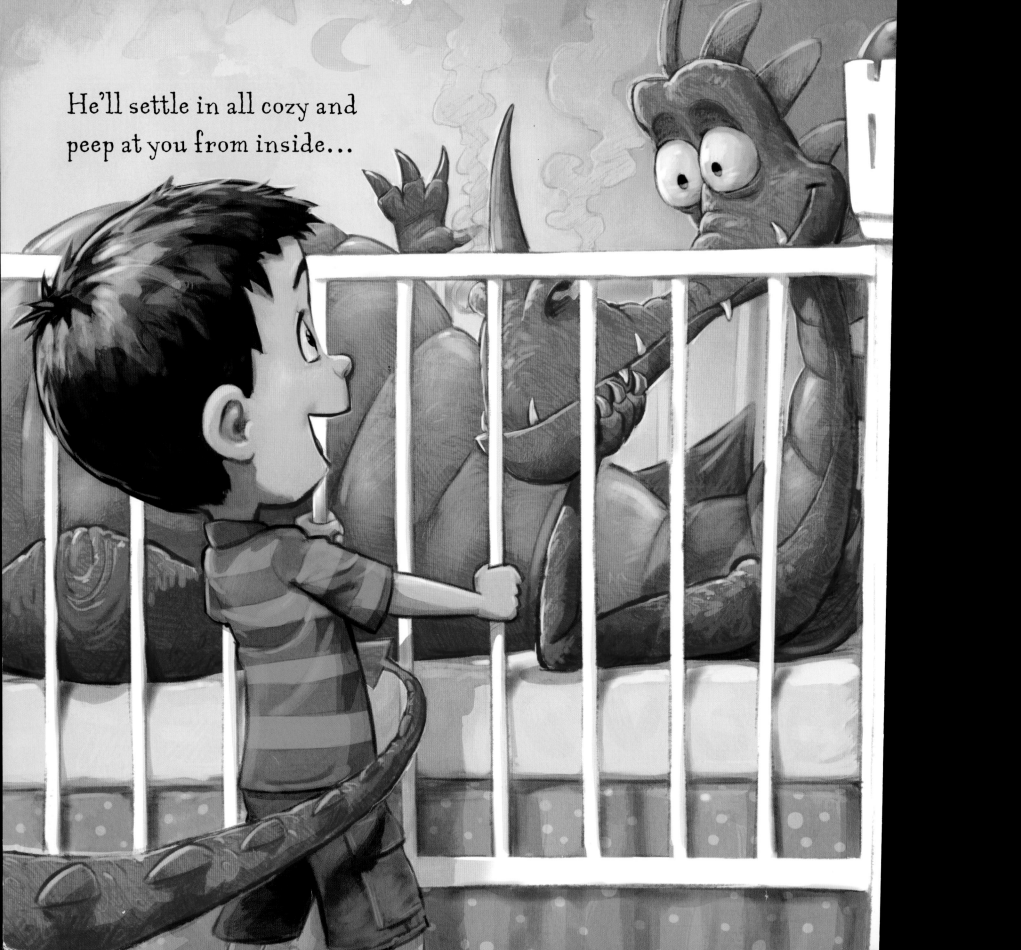

...and you'll wonder how you ever got so lucky.

Until –

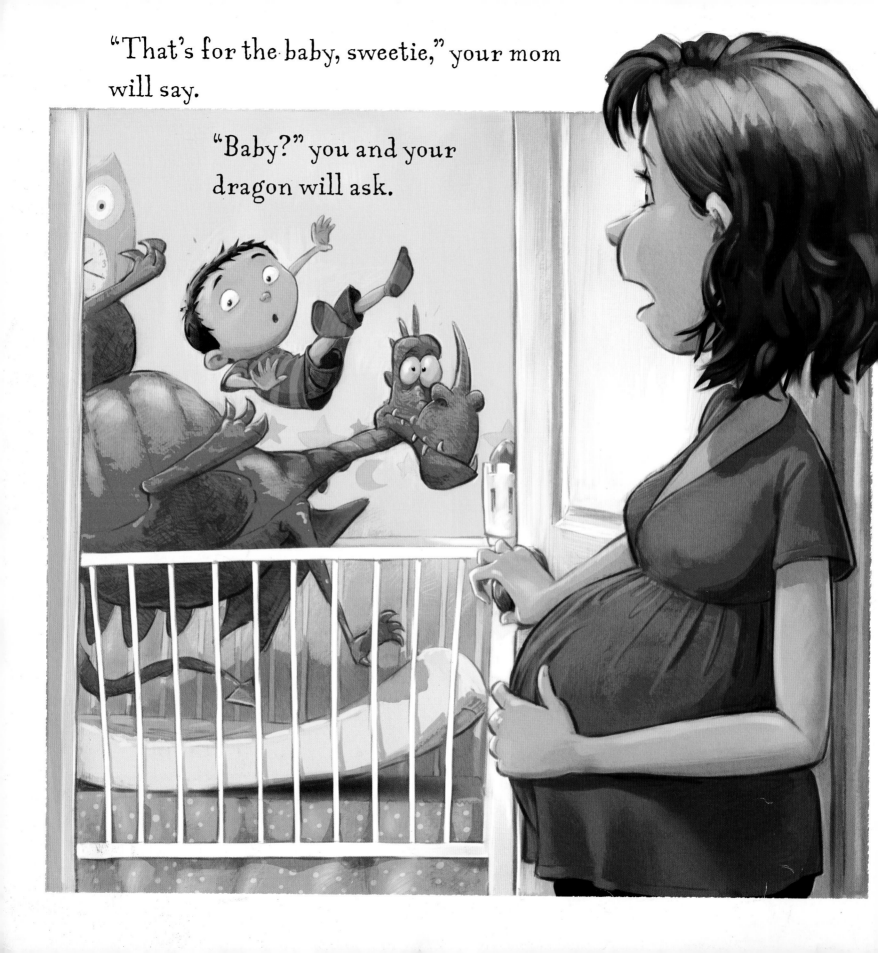

"That's for the baby, sweetie," your mom will say.

"Baby?" you and your dragon will ask.

"Remember?" your dad will say. "You'll be the big brother."

"I hope it's a girl," your sister will add.

Your mom will pat her swelling belly.
"Feel the baby move," she'll say.

"Babies like music,"
your dad will explain.

So you and your dragon will sing your favorite song for the baby – again and again and again.

"I really hope it's a girl," your sister will mutter.

One day, the baby will arrive.

He'll look like you.

"These are not toys," your mom will say.

The baby will giggle.
Your parents
will not.

"It wasn't me,"
you'll explain.
"It was the dragon."

And you'll hear a *heh-heh-heh*
from behind
the couch.

"Lunchtime!"
your dad will say.

So your sister will make
peanut butter sandwiches.

"Dragons don't eat crusts,"
you'll grumble.

"There's no
such thing
as a dragon,"
she'll say.

Your dragon will snicker again –

heh-
heh-
heh

– and accidentally spill juice on her.

"Naptime!" your dad will announce.

"Not for me!" you'll say.
"Naps are for babies.
Not for big boys
        like me and my...

...dragon?"

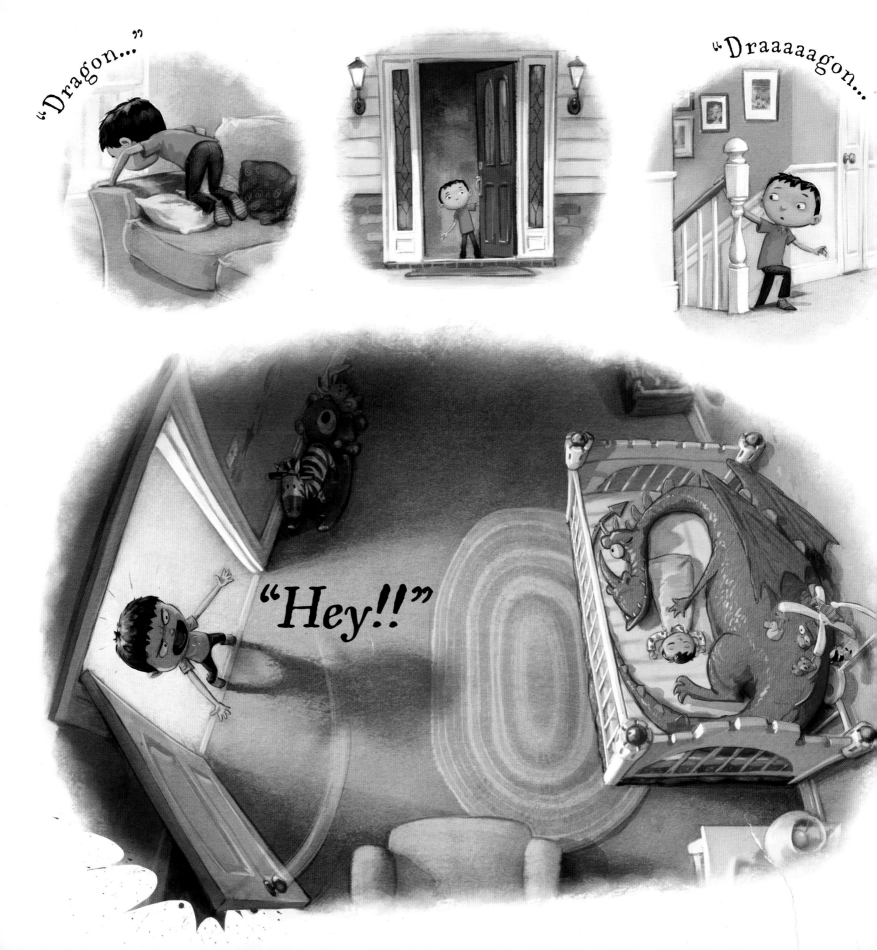

"Young man, I think we've had enough of this dragon business," your dad will say.

"And I've had enough of this baby business!" you'll yell.

Instead, they'll send you to Time Out.

But you won't care.

You don't need that baby.

Or that dragon.

You still have your books...

...and your blocks...

...and your blanket.

Which happens to be your
dragon's blanket, too.

You'll wonder
if he misses it.

Perhaps
you should
check.

"WAH! WAH!" the baby will cry.

"Hush, baby," you'll whisper.

You'll pat his tummy.

He'll burp and
cry some more.

You'll plunk his pacifier into his mouth.

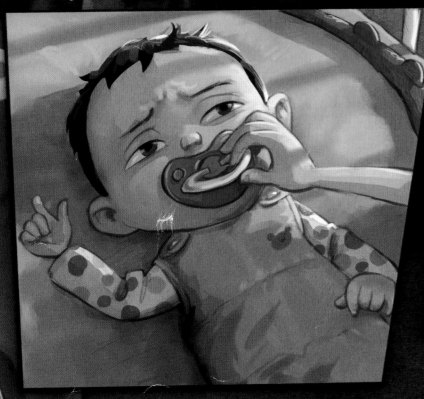

He'll pop it out and cry again.

Finally, you'll remember – babies like music!

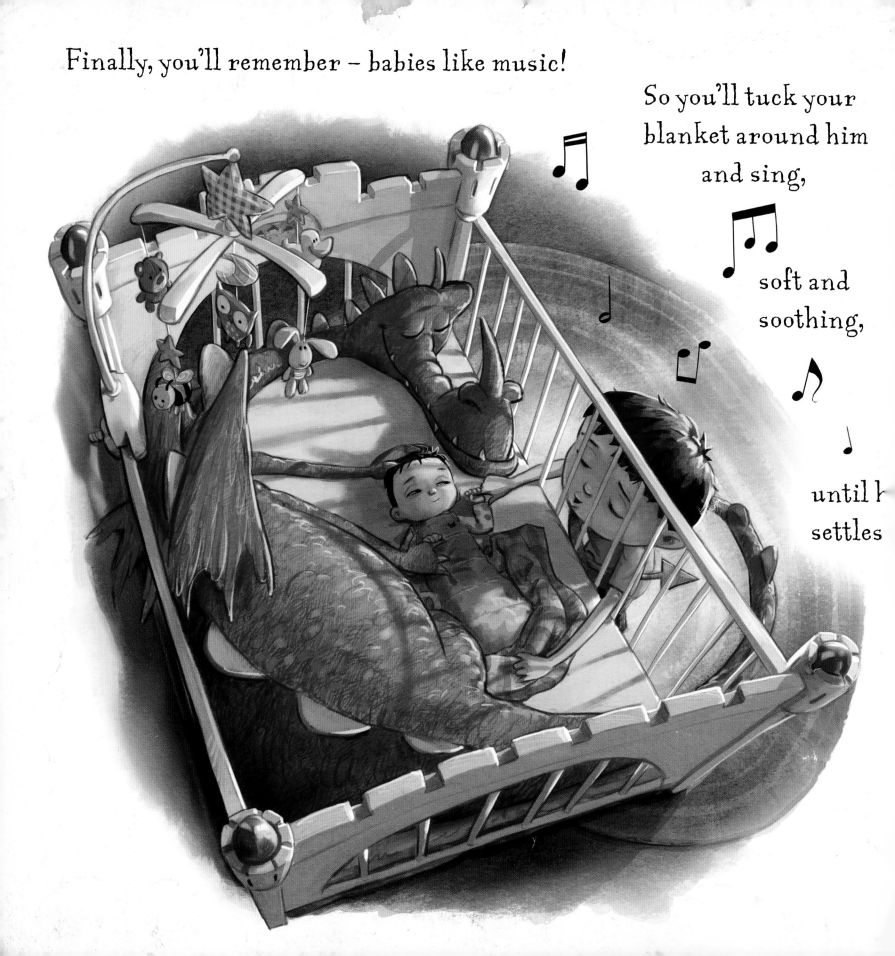

So you'll tuck your blanket around him and sing,

soft and soothing,

until h settles

And you'll decide that
this baby can stay.

At least until tomorrow.

SHOPPING LIST

Baby wipes
Shampoo
Bubble bath
New pacifier
More drool bibs!
Burp cloths